WENDY IN WINTER

By Kaye Starbird

Illustrated by Annie White

HOUGHTON MIFFLIN COMPANY

BOSTON

ATLANTA   DALLAS   GENEVA, ILLINOIS   PALO ALTO   PRINCETON

No wonder Wendy's coat blew off.

She didn't have it zipped.

And – since she didn't watch for slush –

no wonder Wendy slipped.

No wonder Wendy froze her feet,

although her boots were lined,

because when Wendy left for school

she left her boots behind.

And since she didn't dodge the ice

that sagged an apple bough,

no wonder Wendy's hatless head

has seven stitches now.